Last-But-N_____east

LOLA

AND A **KNOT** THE SIZE OF TEXAS

Last-But-Not-Least

LOLA

AND A KNOT THE SIZE OF TEXAS

Christine Pakkala PICTURES BY Paul Hoppe

BOYDS MILLS PRESS

AN IMPRINT OF HIGHLIGHTS

Honesdale, Pennsylvania

Boyds Mills Press
An Imprint of Highlights
815 Church Street
Honesdale, Pennsylvania 18431
boydsmillspress.com

Printed in the United States of America

ISBN: 978-1-62979-324-5 (hc) • 978-1-62979-890-5 (pb) • 978-1-62979-745-8 (eBook)
Library of Congress Control Number: 2016932219
First paperback edition, 2018
The text of this book is set in ITC Novarese Std.
The drawings are done in pen on paper, with digital shading.
10 9 8 7 6 5 4 3 2 1

For Aunt Sue
—CP

For Piotr
—PH

THE KIDS IN MRS. DEBENEDETTI'S SECOND GRADE CLASS (ALPHABETICAL ORDER)

Amanda Anderson

Harvey Baxter

Dilly Chang

Jessie Chavez

Abby Frank

Charlie Henderson

Sam Noonan

Sophie Nunez

Olivia O'Donnell

Madison Rogers

Rita Rohan

Ari Shapiro

Ruby Snow

Jamal Stevenson

Gwendolyn Swanson-Carmichael

John Carmine Tabanelli

Timo Toivonen

Savannah Travers

Ben Wexler

Lola Zuckerman

CONTENTS

1. HUSH ABOUT THE BRIGHT BLUE BRUSH

MY NAME IS LOLA ZUCKERMAN, and Zuckerman means I'm always last. Just like zippers, zoom, and zebras. Last. Zilch, zeroes, and zombies.

ZZZZZZ when you're too tired to stay awake. *ZZZZZZZZ* when a bee is about to sting you. Z. Ding-dong LAST in the alphabet.

"FOR THE LOVE OF PETE!" I yell.

"Lola, don't cuss on the bus!" Amanda says. "Now, HOLD STILL, I told you."

"Yeah, Lola, hold still," Jessie says. "You've got the WORST hair knot I've ever seen."

I hold still, all right. If I don't, Amanda Anderson might just pull all the hair right out of my head.

"I . . . almost . . . almost . . . almost—"

"YOWCH!" I yell. "Stop that, Amanda!" I smooth down the big hair knot on the back of my head. "That's good enough."

"Nuh-uh," Amanda says. "It's stuck in there. Your mom will get it out for you I bet."

"No, sir," I say. "Right before the second grade play she almost killed my whole head." Mom has a bright blue brush that can make curly hair straight.

It can turn a poodle into a collie. That bright blue brush and I are best enemies.

"Amanda, what did your mom say about adopting cats?" Jessie asks. She turns to me. "Amanda wants to adopt brand new deluxe rescue cats."

"I know that," I say. "Remember? Amanda told us last week at our Morning Meeting." I think about fibbing that we're getting some rescue cats, too. And a rescue guinea pig and a rescue horse. Plus some rescue chickens. But I still remember fibbing about getting Savannah Travers a brand-new puppy. So I keep my trap shut.

Except I ask: "Did your mom say yes?"

"She said no," Amanda says.

Sal pulls our bus up to Amanda and Jessie's stop.

Amanda's mom and Jessie's grandma are waiting. Mrs. Anderson has a hold of Barkley, and Jessie's grandma has Maizy, Jessie's purebred West Highland Terrier. I have a burp in my heart 'cause I feel bad that Patches is the only dog at our bus stop. He's all by his lonesome self.

"BYE, AMANDA!" I yell before she climbs off the bus.

"Bye, Lola," she says.

"Bye, Jessie," I say.

Pretty soon it's my stop.

"*Adiós, amiga*," Sal calls.

Mom waves to Sal. She's in her car at the bus stop. Shucks. That means errands.

I stomp over to Mom's car and knock on her window. *RRRR*. Down it goes.

"Get in, Lola Lou," Mom says.

"Why is Jack in the front seat?"

Jack leans forward and gives me a Jack-o-Lantern smile. "Because I'm a big kid."

"Remember, Lola?" Mom asks.

I'm not tall enough for the front seat, even though I stretch myself every night. I climb into the backseat right next to a big bolt of fabric and buckle myself up. "Where are we going?"

"Shopping."

I groan. "For clothes?" All those itchy tags and sales ladies—*blech*! I don't like shopping for clothes. No, sir.

Mom says. "No, food shopping. And I have a surprise."

"What-what-what?" I ask.

"I was going to wait to tell you, but Granny thought . . . ," Mom says.

Jack answers, "Granny and Grampy Coogan are coming for Thanksgiving. When they went home this summer and you bawled your eyes out . . ."

"I did not!"

"They bought tickets and kept it a big surprise," Jack informs me.

"Then how do you know?" I ask Jack.

He just shrugs. "I'm older. I know stuff."

"They thought we would *all* enjoy their company," Mom says.

I forget about mad. "They're coming?" I hop up and down in my seat.

"In three days," Mom says.

"Grandma's still coming, too? Right, Mom?"

"That's right," Mom says.

"Are we having olives?" Jack says. "I'm going to put one olive on every finger and eat them off."

"Me, too!" I hop up and down, up and down, like I do on Jack's pogo stick when he says I can use it.

Then my hop stops.

I think of something bad about having ALL those grandparents at Thanksgiving.

My grandmas ALWAYS ask me and Jack TWO HORRIBLE QUESTIONS. "How do you like my pumpkin pie? Is it the best pumpkin pie you ever tasted?"

It's like being the rope in a tug-of-war game.

Jack told me to tell BOTH of them their pie is the best. I know that's lying. I know one is better.

I know one tastes like licking a candle. I'm not telling which. So I lie to one of those grannies. Now both grannies are going to be in one place. My house. What if they find out I'm lying? What if I get caught?

Lying is bad. And so is getting caught.

2. SHOPPING AT SWIRLYS

BEFORE MOM CAN DRIVE OFF,
two faces pop up outside the car. One is white
and wrinkly (that's Mrs. McCracken, our next door
neighbor) and the other is white and fluffy (that's
Dwight White, her cat).

I roll down my window.

"Hello!" Mom says. "How are—"

"I saw you parked here, so I came to ask—please
keep Patches out of my yard! He was digging in my
flower bed and doing his business on my grass

and scaring poor Dwight White again."

"Oh, my goodness!" Mom squeaks. "I am so sorry . . ."

But Mrs. McCracken just marches away with Dwight White peeking over her shoulder.

Mom drums her hand on the steering wheel before we pull away. I just know I'm about to get in BIG trouble. On account of the fact that walking Patches is my job. And sometimes he sees Jeremy Squirrel and takes off running. Right into Mrs. McCracken's No-Dog zone. I tried to tell Mrs. McCracken that Patches is best friends with Jeremy Squirrel. She said fine but could they be friends in our backyard?

Mom sighs. "Kids," she says as she drives down the road. "This is a problem. What do you suggest we do about it?"

"Maybe we could get Patches a treadmill," Jack says.

"That's not happening," Mom says.

"We should keep Patches on a leash and never let him off even when he pulls so hard your arm is about to pop out of its socket," I say.

"Well, I wouldn't do that," Mom says. "But I think the two of you need to come up with a solution."

"Maybe I should walk Patches all the time, and Lola has to pick up the dog doo in the yard all the time," Jack suggests. "Dog doo can't get away from you."

"No thanks," I say.

"All right," Mom says. "You two can work this out later. But just remember, Patches . . ."

"Is our responsibility," I say.

We bump down North Avenue. I read the

Thanksgiving menu that Dad made.

- DAD: TURKEY AND SECRET CHESTNUT
  STUFFING, BUTTERNUT SQUASH PUREE,
  MASHED POTATOES, BROCCOLI WITH A
  CHEESE SAUCE, SALAD
- MOM: DINNER ROLLS AND OLIVES
- GRANNY AND GRAMPY COOGAN: PUMPKIN PIE
- GRANDMA: PUMPKIN PIE

"Why is Dad making the broccoli with a cheese sauce? And the secret stuffing?"

"Remember?" Mom asks. "What we talked about last night? Big Lola dress order due just after Thanksgiving?"

"Maybe Lola got thunked on the head at recess and now she has amnesia," Jack says. "And she can't even remember her own name."

"No, sir. My name is Lola Zuckerman."

"How can you be sure?"

"Jack," Mom says with a "one" tucked into her voice. Three means big trouble. "Lola, remember?"

I sigh with extra breath so she can hear me loud and clear. "You have to sew twelve Lola dresses."

"Yes, that's right, Lola. Let's get back to our list. What else would make Thanksgiving wonderful?"

"You not working so much," Jack grumps out.

"Cranberry sauce!" I say.

"Ooh, glad you remembered," Mom says.

I take out my watermelon-smelling pencil from

my pencil pocket. I add "cranberry sauce" to the bottom of the list. I love the way cranberry sauce is shaped like a can.

"What are we doing here?" I pipe up. It's not Swirlys.

"You tell her, Mom," Jack says. And he hops out.

We wait for Jack to ring the bell. A lady I never even met waves at us before she lets him inside. Mom waves back. On the drive to Swirlys Mom tells me that Jack has an after-school job babysitting for that lady.

"But he doesn't even like medium-sized kids like me," I say.

"You know Jack loves you," Mom says. Fishsticks.

Mom turns into Swirlys's parking lot. I skip over to the carts, pull one out, and ride it up to Mom.

Right inside the store is a big display of flowers. Mom stops in front of them. "Lola, did you go to school with your hair like that?" She tries to smooth my hair down with her hand.

"Sort of. But it picked up gusto during the day."

"You'll have to

give it a good brushing tonight," Mom says, and I wince. Wince is when you worry and squint at the same time.

"Now, let's see," Mom says while she's looking over the flowers. "Would you like to choose three bunches? We can make a nice Thanksgiving centerpiece. While you're doing that, I'm going to grab some onions."

I choose some orange roses, some yellow lilies, and some red carnations. I know lots of flower names 'cause Granny Coogan taught me. Just when I'm sniffing a real smelly plant, somebody pokes me.

"Hi, Lola!" Jessie Chavez says.

"Hi, Jessie!" We do our secret Tomato and Swiss Cheese handshake.

"I sure hate shopping," Jessie says. "It's bo-oring."

"Me, too," I say. We act like zombies until the flower lady zings us with a Mean Slicer look.

"Uh-oh. Your hair is boinking up over there," Jessie says.

I pat my head. "These are just some springy
curls," I tell her.

"Jessie," her granny calls from the stack of
bananas.

"Gotta go!" she says. "That's going to hurt really
bad to get that knot out."

"No sir, IT WON'T!" I say, only it gets out of control into a yell.

Everyone stops. Everyone turns. Everyone looks shocked. That was loud.

Mom marches over. "Lola!" She yell-whispers. "No shouting."

Fishsticks.

If you see Jessie Chavez coming, you better hide.

She'll get you all worried about a teensy little hair knot that won't hurt at all when you brush it. Not one bit.

3. TALLY MARK, GET SET, GO HOME

"WHAT'S UP WITH THE BASE-
ball cap?" Dad asks me at the bus stop the next
day.

"It might rain," I say.

Dad looks up at the sky. The sun is shining, big
and yellow like a sunny-side up egg. Dad says it's
the warmest day ever on record just two days from
Thanksgiving. Granny Coogan says it's so hot down
in Texas the hens are laying hard-boiled eggs. She
can't wait to get on an airplane in two days and

come up here where hens lay regular eggs.

"Lola," Dad says. "Tell me the truth."

I think fast. "Dad, what's the difference between happy and happy-go-lucky?"

"Happy is Patches wagging his tail when he gets a treat. Happy-go-lucky is when he doesn't get a treat, but he *still* wags his tail."

"Oh." I need another idea quick. "Aren't you

sad Chuncle's not coming for Thanksgiving?" I ask. Chuncle is my Uncle Charlie.

Dad looks pensive. Pensive means you're sad and you wish you had a pen to write it down. "Yes, I am," Dad says. "I don't get to see Chuncle nearly as often as I'd like."

"Did you play Blanket of Doom with him when you were kids?" I ask.

Dad smiles. "Maybe not that game, but lots of other games."

"But then you got to be big and you had to stop," I say. And that gets me thinking.

"And the hat?" Dad asks again because he's good at remembering.

"I forgot to brush my hair under here," I say.

"Hmm," Dad says. But the bus pulls up before Dad's "hmm" can get somewhere.

On the bus I take off my baseball cap and scratch my head. Whew. I sit down and wave to Dad. Dad waves goodbye to me. Suddenly, Dad frowns. He points to my head.

I read Dad's lips. "Your hair!" he's shouting. He
pretends to brush his head.

"HUH?" I play dumb. 'Cause last night I just
glided my brush over the top layer. That sneaky
snarly knot hid underneath like a mean ol'
tumbleweed. Mom wasn't watching me brush my
hair good 'cause her sewing machine was bunching
up all her thread. Plus, I was in a hurry to get to
bed 'cause Dad was telling me the next installment
of "Adventures of Dad and Chuncle" (and it was
a good one, 'cause Chuncle got stuck in a heating

vent). I guess that smooth top layer did a good hiding job. Dad didn't notice the sneaking stinker knot.

Now it's big as a tennis ball. I try to smooth it down. I wave goodbye to Dad. He's still pretend-brushing away at his head.

Jessie and Amanda get on the bus.

"You never brushed your hair, did you?" Jessie points out first thing.

"Maybe I did and maybe I didn't," I say.

"You didn't," Jessie says.

Amanda doesn't say anything. She's looking kind of soupy.

At school, they go into the bathroom to brush their hair. I barrel straight to my classroom because I love being first in the room. And I love Mrs. D. And there she is, sharpening pencils. She LOVES sharp pencils.

"HI, MRS. D." I shout to get her attention. "I'm here FIRST!"

"Good morning, Lola," Mrs. D. says in her Milk voice. "You are early, aren't you?"

"Yep, 'cause Sal drives really fast."

"Well, he follows the speed limit, I'm sure," Mrs. D. says.

"Sal told me that his wife is making bittersweet chocolate pudding cake with vanilla gelato for Thanksgiving."

Mrs. D. smacks her lips. "Yum! I'd like to taste that!"

"How 'bout homemade cranberry sauce?" I ask. "We're making that."

"Homemade?" she says. "That would be nice."

"Ours is can-shaped," I tell her.

Also: "I can tell it's going to be a good day."

"Glad to hear it," she says.

I wait for her to ask me why.

And wait. And wait.

She's slurping down her coffee from her travel mug and reading something.

"Wanna know why?" I FINALLY ask.

"Why?"

"'Cause it's Tally Mark Tuesday."

"Oh! You like tally marks, don't you, Lola?"

I nod really hard so she gets my point. "They look like four people carrying one person who fell down and broke her leg."

"Hmm, I suppose so," she says.

First I go through my Morning Routine. I sign up for the hot lunch today because it's ziti. *Ziti* starts with a Z and goes last just like *Zuckerman*. Poor poor poor ziti. I pass in my homework.

I look up at the bulletin board. The bulletin board is handy in case you ever forget the month. Up there a turkey's wearing a Pilgrim's hat.

Soon the classroom is filled with all the kids in Mrs. D.'s class. I have a whole lot of love inside me. So I hug Savannah Travers in her rainbow T-shirt. I hug Olivia in her fuzzy pink sweater. I hug Madison in her purple silk kimono all the way from Tokyo, Japan. And Amanda Anderson finally gets done looking in the mirror and I hug her and I can tell she still feels soupy. I smile our Super Goofer Smile. But Amanda doesn't smile back.

"What's wrong, Amanda?" I ask. I pat her on her head real careful so I don't give her a hair knot.

But Amanda just shakes her head. "Nothing,"

she says, and it sounds like she forgot how to say "everything."

Gwendolyn Swanson-Carmichael comes in. "Lola, your dress has too many pockets," she tells me.

"No, sir!" I say. "This is my brand-new Lola dress my mom made me with deluxe pockets." Deluxe means you wish you had one. Mom made twenty-eight for those people in California and one extra special one for me. It's got every color in the rainbow 'cause I don't like to play favorites.

"Well, I still think . . . ," Gwendolyn Swanson-Carmichael says.

I growl at her like Patches 'cause I ran out of nice. She runs away.

Harvey Baxter hangs off the back of his chair, and Ari Shapiro falls flat on the carpet 'cause he got shot by the Green Lord.

"Good morning, Gumdrops!" Mrs. D. calls. "Harvey, Ari, up." She gulps coffee from her travel mug.

After morning meeting, it's time for Math, which means time for the Tally Mark Activity. My leg is going jigger jigger jigger 'cause it's ready for recess even though the rest of me can't wait for tally marks.

On one side of the chalkboard, Mrs. D. writes, "Traveling for Thanksgiving." On the other side, she writes, "Staying Home for Thanksgiving."

I can't wait to add my tally to the side that says, "Staying Home for Thanksgiving." But with the name Zuckerman, I will go last. Dead last.

Mrs. D. stands there with a piece of chalk ready for action. "Amanda, you're first."

"We're going to Cancún, Mexico," Amanda says.
Amanda's eyes get all shiny. Mrs. D. makes a tally

mark under "Traveling for Thanksgiving." A tear leaks right out of Amanda's eye.

"What's wrong, Amanda?" I ask in my loudest whisper.

"Nothing," Amanda whispers back. But it's something all right 'cause Amanda says, "I don't want to go to Cancún for Thanksgiving!" loud enough that the whole class hears her.

"You don't?" Jessie says. "But that's a deluxe vacation destination."

"Oh, dear!" Mrs. D. says. "I'm sorry to hear that."

Before I can holler, "There, there," like a grown-up, Amanda runs right out of the room. And it wasn't even my fault.

"Lola, go follow her!" Mrs. D. tells me, even though Mrs. D. loves people sitting down. I spring up from my desk and zip after Amanda.

4. STALL NUMBER THREE

I RUN OUT INTO THE HALLWAY.

I look right. No Amanda. I look left. No Amanda.

I run-skip down the hall. Here comes Señora Weinstein.

"Lola, ¿cómo estás?" Señora Weinstein asks. That means, "How are you?" in Spanish.

I pause. I wish I knew how to say in Spanish, "I'm fine except I'm looking for my friend Amanda, and she's not fine. She's sad about Thanksgiving. She doesn't want to go to Cancún."

"*Estoy bien*," I say instead.

"Blah, blah, blah," Señora Weinstein says in Spanish.

I curtsy. That seems like a Spanish thing to do. "Adiós, amiga," I say. I hurry on down to the girls' bathroom and swing open the door wide.

"YOO HOO?" I yell in there. It's okay to yell 'cause I'm looking for somebody.

Drip-drip and *clank-clank*. And that's it. Not even a flush.

"Amanda?" I call out. "Amanda?"

No answer.

"Amanda, we might be missing Tally Mark Day."

No answer. Fishsticks. Maybe Amanda isn't in here.

I crouch and look under Stall Number One. No Amanda there. I look under Stall Number Two. No Amanda. I lean under Stall Number Three. There's Amanda, sitting with her feet pulled off the ground.

I smile up at Amanda. "Hi, Amanda!"

"Hello." Even when Amanda is sad, she's polite.

"Amanda, are you coming out of there?"

Amanda shakes her head no.

"Amanda, aren't you afraid to miss Tally Mark Day?"

Amanda's feet plunk down, and I scooch out of the way. She opens the stall door, and I stand up. I'm glad she came out. I was getting a crick in my neck.

But Amanda looks funny. Not ha-ha funny. Mad funny.

"Lola Zuckerman! You just said what YOU care about. I don't care about tally marks!"

"Oh," I say. I didn't know that.

"Do you even KNOW why I'm sad?"

I nod really hard. I hope I have the right answer.

"You don't want to go to Cancún for Thanksgiving."
That *is* the right answer because Amanda stops
crying. Or at least she slows down her crying.

"That's right. And last year we went to—"

"The Bahamas," I say.

"And the year before we went to—"

"Florida."

"That's right. You have a good memory, Lola. And
I really want to just stay home and make pumpkin
bread in—"

"Your deluxe new kitchen?"

"I don't care about
the deluxe part, Lola
Zuckerman," Amanda says
kind of huffy. "I care about
never getting to have
Thanksgiving at home. I
want to set the table with
special napkins and make a
big centerpiece that looks
like a turkey."

I'm about to say that I picked out flowers at Swirlys for our centerpiece. But a lucky stop sign in my head shuts my trap up. "What's a centerpiece?" I fib-ask.

"You put it on your table to make it look nice. I want to make everything look fancy like in *Cozy Home* magazine. I want to hang up an autumn wreath and put a bowl of cinnamon-scented pinecones at the front door.

"Oh." I scratch my head and try to look like that sounds fun.

"But I can't because my mom and dad always want to go on vacation to some place where it's hot and there are beaches and drinks with umbrellas."

"I only go to the beach in the summer," I say. But then I think of something terrible. Something worse

than Grandma's goulash. "You'll have to keep Barkley at the dog hotel while you're gone," I blurt. "He won't get any scraps at all. That's what happened to Patches, and boy was he lonesome." My mouth keeps going on even though my eyeballs see Amanda's face getting kind of squinched.

"I never thought of that," she says in a whisper like an old dead leaf blowing in the breeze. She starts crying a little. And then she starts crying a lot. Amanda's crying gets really loud like a blow-dryer.

I feel more rotten than the banana Mom found in Jack's sock drawer. (And how it got there, she'll never know.)

"Don't cry, Amanda! I know! Barkley can stay with

us," I say. "We're hosting Thanksgiving this year."

Amanda sniffs. "He can?"

"Sure! He and Patches will have a blast!"

"Your mom won't mind?" Amanda has part of a smile on her face. She knows, and I know, all about Mom. Mom cares about animals. She cares about hugging, and flowers, and sewing up Lola dresses and other stuff on her sewing machine. She even sewed up a dog bed for Patches two whole times 'cause he ate the first one.

I remember what Mom said about walking Patches. I can barely hold on to Patches. How am I going to hold on to two rascal dogs? I think of all that dog doo Jack will make me clean up.

But I have to make Amanda's half smile a whole one. "Mom loves dogs," I say. I make a panting dog face. Amanda laughs.

"She'll probably make Barkley his own dog bed. And matching outfits for Patches and Barkley!" I smile big at Amanda. Amanda smiles big at me. Amanda and I jump up and down 'cause we're so excited about those matching outfits.

"Do you feel better?" I pat Amanda on the back. Amanda nods.

"Well, except that I won't get to decorate the table like in *Cozy Home*."

Ding-dang quick, I say, "Christmas is just around the corner. You're not going away for that, are you?"

"Oh no!" Amanda says. "My grandparents are coming, and we're going to make a gingerbread house!"

"Just think of how fancy you can set *that* table," I say. "I bet you will make the most loveliest centerpiece."

And do you know what Amanda does? She grabs a hold of me and gives me the biggest hug a friend ever got.

"You'd better rinse your face off," I tell her. Amanda goes to the sink, and so do I. Above my head is a kind of hat. Made out of hair.

"Oh!" I say.

I turn sideways. In the back of my head the knot is sticking straight out.

"Wow," Amanda says, her face dripping wet. "How did you do that?"

"It's easy," I say. "I haven't brushed my hair for thirteen days."

And only I know why I haven't brushed my hair for thirteen days.

4½. WHY I HAVEN'T BRUSHED MY HAIR FOR THIRTEEN DAYS

OKAY. I'LL TELL YOU.

Amanda brushes her hair every single night. She washes it with Love A Lot Apricot Shampoo and conditions it with Mango Fandango Conditioner.

I wash and condition my hair, too. But when it comes to brushing it, my arm goes wobbly like an old tired snake. I've got a big mess of curls on my head that I'll be glad to have someday. But not today. And not yesterday or the day before.

One time, Mom was in a hurry and she took her special brush and raked right through a knot in my hair. It hurt really bad, and I screamed my head off and I had to go sit in my room and write I WILL NOT SCREAM IN MOM'S EAR ten times.

That was thirteen days ago.

Ever since then, Mom hands me the brush after my bath and says, "Now, Lola, it's time for *you* to brush *your* hair."

I brush my hair. I DO! But the brush only works on the outside. The brush doesn't go inside to the really bad hair. It stays bad under there. And no one can tell.

So I don't mention it.

But now I have a knot in the back of my head the size of a biggish fruit. Not a cantaloupe, but maybe a navel orange.

5. TALLY HO!

"GOOD, YOU'RE BACK," MRS. D. says. "Did you solve the problem?"

"Yes, we did," Amanda says. "Lola made me feel better. She reminded me that Christmas is just around the corner, and I'll get to set the table really fancy and hang a wreath and trim the tree. And she said my dog can stay at her house for Thanksgiving."

"Oh. Did you say that, Lola?"

"Yes," I say.

"Wonderful," Mrs. D. says. But the *wonderful*

doesn't sound so wonderful. It sounds worryful.

"Lola, you've got a hair knot," Timo Toivonen calls down from the reading loft.

Amanda grabs two colored pencils and sticks them right in my hair knot. "In America, we call it a hair bun," she says.

"Now let's come together, Candy Corns," Mrs. D. says. "The class wanted to pause the tally mark activity so that everyone could participate."

Inside I'm doing cartwheels 'cause I LUH-HUV tally marks.

Everyone takes a seat. On my way, Savannah shows me her book about fairy people with wings. I say I like the bald, green fairy. Bald fairies don't get hair knots.

Mrs. D. says, "Now, Harvey, how about you?"

"I'm going to Ohio," Harvey says. "I wish I was going to Cancún."

Mrs. D. puts his tally mark on the board. Dilly is next, and she's traveling to Chinatown in New York City to be with her grandparents.

Jessie stands up to make her Tally Mark announcement. "I have a spectacular surprise," she says. "My parents, and my grandma, and even my brother, Dustin, are all traveling to—" she smiles at the whole class, "—Barbados. That's a tropical paradise."

The whole class oohs and ahhs. "Yay," I say, only my *yay* ran out of fizz like flat root beer. Amanda's going to Cancún, Savannah's going to California, and Jessie's going to a tropical paradise. All I'm going to is the kitchen to help load the dishwasher.

But then I remember how I love can-shaped cranberry sauce from scratch. And just like that I cheer myself up.

I daydream of cranberry sauce through a bunch of the alphabet.

"In Finland," Timo Toivonen says, "we don't celebrate Thanksgiving. Thanksgiving is an American holiday."

"So you won't celebrate?" Sam calls out.

"Hand, Sam," Mrs. D. says.

"We will celebrate our Finnish version at home," Timo Toivonen says. "We call it Kiitospäivä."

The whole class repeats it: KEY TOES PIE VA.
Mrs. D. makes a tally mark under "Staying Home for
Thanksgiving."

Savannah Travers gets up. She waves to me and I
wave to her. "I'm going on an airplane to Manhattan
Beach, California, and I'm going to play with all my
cousins!"

She gives me a big smile. I stretch one across my
lips. Something in me feels wince-y. But then I give
myself a pep talk because I'm going to be happy
making cranberry sauce from scratch. I'm going to
be happy eating two pumpkin pies. I'm going to be
happy as a kid on a beach. A warm beach where
kids are building sand castles right in the middle of
November. Fishsticks.

Ben Wexler is traveling all the way to Lewiston,
Maine.

Finally, Z! Finally me!

Mrs. D. stands up straight and puts Ben's tally
mark on the side of "Traveling on Thanksgiving." But

when she turns around, she has a big white chalk mark across her rear end.

We burst out laughing. Mrs. D. looks over her shoulder. "Oh, my!" she says, and gives her rear end a good dusting off.

I glance at the clock. It's time for Snack. Mrs. D. will have to hurry.

"Last but not least, we have Lola. What are you doing, Lola?"

Fishsticks. I've been waiting all day and all night and part of another day to say, "Staying at home." But now staying at home sounds bo-oring.

"Staying at home," I say in the world's smallest voice.

Mrs. D. wrinkles up her brow like a bulldog. Then she says. "Oh. Staying at home." She adds my tally mark to the Staying At Home kids. I'm the broken-leg kid being carried by the other four.

"Who would like to tally up the marks?" Mrs. D. asks.

Hands shoot up. Not mine. Mine are two pieces of the most cooked-up spaghetti you'd ever want to see. Mrs. D. calls on Rita Rohan.

"Fifteen kids are traveling and five are staying home," she says.

"My goodness! How exciting! Snack time!"

6. STUCK LIKE A BULLFROG

MISS NIMBY COMES IN TO MAKE sure we don't get frisky while Mrs. D. leaves the room to refill her travel mug with coffee.

"Remember to use your napkins," she says. "I'll be back in a jiffy."

Jessie skips on up to my desk. "Lola, can you watch Maizy, too? She's supposed to stay at the dog groomer's, but she would be so happy to be with her friends."

For a second (or one hundred seconds) I want

to say no, sir because Maizy always gets playdates with Barkley, and Patches never does. But then I don't, because Maizy will be lonesome, and I'll have a sick, green heart.

Mrs. D. sweeps back into the room with her travel mug. She writes, "Writers' Workshop" on the board.

"All right, Fruit Tarts, today we're going to write Personal Narratives all about our Thanksgivings. We're going to answer the question *What are you thankful about at Thanksgiving?*"

Then Mrs. D. hands out one of her special writing rubrics. That's a chart to show us how to do a good job. Mrs. D. says we need to have a main idea and at least three details.

Gwendolyn raises her hand. "How many details do we need to do the best job ever?"

Mrs. D. takes a swig of her coffee from her travel coffee mug. "Gwendolyn, try to choose the best details for your narrative. Are you thankful for your turkey dinner? If so, how would you describe a turkey dinner at your home?"

Rita Rohan raises her hand. "Mrs. D., my family is vegetarian. We don't eat turkey."

"We have turkey *and* pumpkin tortelloni," John Carmine Tabanelli calls.

"We eat roast duck," Olivia says.

"It's not Thanksgiving if you don't have turkey," Harvey belts out.

"Yes, it is so," I holler.

"Is it Thanksgiving if you don't serve turkey?" Mrs. D. asks us.

I snap up my hand. "Yes, because last year we had Thanksgiving in Texas at a restaurant when

Granny Coogan's oven conked out. But it was still Thanksgiving."

"I see," Mrs. D. says. "So whether or not we have turkey, we still have Thanksgiving—as long as we have things to be thankful for. And I believe we all have things to be thankful for. Don't we, Sweet Tarts?"

"You're teaching us a lesson," Harvey says.

Gwendolyn raises her hand. "I have some details about turkey for *my* Personal Narrative because I'm thankful we have that for *our* Thanksgiving. Moist, tasty, juicy, delicious, flavorful, yummy, and tasty."

"She said 'tasty' twice," Sam yells.

"She took ALL the good details," Madison cries.

"Those details can be used by everyone," Mrs. D. says. "Well done, Gwendolyn. Gummy Bears, let's get down to business and start writing our Personal Narratives."

I get out my watermelon-smelling pencil and my purple notebook.

I am thankful . . .

But my tankful of thankful just ran out of gas.

Jessie and Amanda *and* Savannah are going somewhere exciting and fun for Thanksgiving. I'm going nowhere but home, stuck like a bullfrog in a mud pond.

With two dogs that Mom doesn't know about yet. Two dogs that Mrs. McCracken doesn't know about either.

7. GLUM CHUM

THE WHOLE CLASS SAYS GOOD-
bye and Happy Thanksgiving to Jessie. That's
because she's going to Barbados tomorrow. And
not to school. Poor ol' Amanda has to go shopping
for bathing suits. Mrs. Anderson picks her up after
school, so I get to sit with Jessie on the bus ride
home. We play Miss Mary Mack and we do the Hand
Jive.

I forget all about being sad until Jessie says,
"Thank you for watching Maizy. Bammy and I will
bring her over later, okay?"

"Okay," I say.

Sal rumbles up to Jessie's stop. There's her grandma, all right, with Maizy wagging her tail. I can't let Maizy down.

"Bye, Lola!" Jessie calls out.

Sal pulls the lever to shut the doors. He turns onto North Avenue.

It's the stop before mine. Four noisy boys get off and suddenly the bus is quiet. Too quiet.

Sal is so lucky. He's bald. He's never going to get a hair knot EVER.

"Sal, do people go bald from brushing knots out of their hair?"

"No," Sal says. He pulls away from the curb.

The next stop is mine. Sal pulls up and opens the door.

Oh no. There's Dad, holding on tight to Patches's leash. Now what? Dad never forgets anything and I bet he's just waiting for me and my hair knot.

"Lola," Dad says as soon as I get off the bus. "Why is your school bag on your head?"

I think fast. "It's hot out here."

"Lola, my dear, darling daughter, I remember that you have a tangle of hair. We're going to need to brush it."

"But that's going to kill my head," I say.

"I highly doubt that."

Dad and Patches and I walk up the road, and I think about running away to a town where nobody combs their hair. But then I'd have to come back in time for Thanksgiving. Patches lifts his leg up right on Mrs. McCracken's rosebush. She sure won't like that and neither will Dwight White. Dad says, "No, Patches!" But Patches doesn't speak good English.

Seeing Patches makes me remember that I have to ask Dad about hosting Barkley and Maizy. I'll ask him when he doesn't look so out of breath.

Dad pulls Patches back. "Patches sure is a handful! We have to make sure we keep him calm during Thanksgiving."

"He'll be calm," I say. "He'll probably sleep through the whole thing."

Dad snorts, and that's not nice.

Jack is shooting hoops in the driveway. Dad hands me Patches's leash and grabs the ball away from Jack. He tosses it towards the hoop. It misses by a mile.

"Try again, Dad! Like this!" Jack sinks it.

Dad tries to throw the basketball in again. *ZLOOP.* It pops right in. Dad high-fives Jack.

"Here, Lola," Jack says. I hand Patches's leash back to Dad, and Jack tosses me the ball. "You try."

I throw the ball. It misses by two miles.

"When you're a big kid, you'll be better," Jack says.

"I am a big kid," I say.

"No, you're not."

"YES, I AM!"

"If you were, you wouldn't be screaming."

I'd better practice acting like a big kid since I'm going to be in charge of a whole bunch of dogs. I try to go in the back door first. I read that you should show the dog you're the boss. You should go through the door first. But Patches goes in first anyway.

Dad puts out bowls of popcorn and cups of cider. "Lola, after this snack, we're going to work on that knot."

Oh no. That's bad. Special Brush bad. Poodle Into Collie bad.

"Why are you eating your popcorn one kernel at a time?" Jack asks me.

"Yes, Lola, why are you?" Dad asks. Then, the phone rings.

"Hello? Yes, this is Mr. Zuckerman. Hello, Mrs. Chavez. Lola told Jessie what?" Dad gets a big, black storm cloud right on his face. He holds up one finger and leaves the kitchen.

I decide that I'm going upstairs and getting that knot out by myself.

But Patches whines right at the door.

"Patches! You have to go AGAIN?" I ask.

Patches says *yes* in dog.

"Your turn," I say.

"You said you could handle Patches," Jack says. "Just like a big kid."

"I can!" I grab Patches's leash and we head out the door.

I'll take care of my knot as soon as I get back to the house. Maybe.

8. DOG-GONE IT!

RIGHT IN THE DRIVEWAY,

Patches pees by our mailbox.

"Good dog!" I pat him. He sits down next to me and his tongue hangs out.

Jeremy Squirrel darts down a tree. Patches yanks the leash right out of my hand and takes off after him. He disappears into a bush.

"No, Patches! Come out of there, you bad dog!"

Suddenly, Patches bounds through the branches. His tail is wagging hard.

"Good dog! Here, Patches!" I smack my hands on my legs in a come-here way.

Patches comes running. "Good boy!" He runs right on by me. "Bad boy!" I chase after him. "Get back here! Now!"

Jack comes into the driveway, twirling his basketball.

"Jack, help me get Patches!"

Jack drops his basketball. "Patches!" he yells, waving his arms around.

Patches stops. His tail is wagging even harder. Jack sneaks forward.

Jack jumps, but Patches jumps too.

Now Patches runs straight towards me. This time I stand like a statue. Patches stops and looks at me with his big brown eyes.

"Ground to air, I repeat, ground to air, we have almost reached the dog," Jack says. He is creeping toward Patches. Patches is crouching just a little, getting ready to zip away. I leap and land right on him.

But Patches wiggles out. He darts all the way down Cherry Tree Lane.

Jack and I race after him, and we keep hollering. Patches stops at the end of our street. Then, just when we're closing in on him, he streaks right past us!

We turn around and go chasing in the other direction.

The new neighbor with a baby waves from her front porch. "Hi, Jack!"

"How do you know the new neighbor?" I huff out.

"I'm going to rake her leaves and make

money to help out Mom and Dad," Jack huffs back.

"But you're already babysitting. No fair!" I wheeze. "I want to help Mom and Dad."

"You can't. You're a little kid." Jack pants. "You don't mean to, but you just cause a lot of trouble."

"I do NOT!"

"Look at all the trouble we're in right now."

"But half is your fault."

"Three quarters is your fault, because you were watching Patches. One quarter is mine, because I should have been watching you."

"No, sir, you shouldn't have," I holler at Jack.

We whiz down to our end of the block just in time to see Patches zip into Mrs. McCracken's yard. "Patches, you bad dog!"

Jack and I chase after Patches. "Not again!" Dirt comes flying out of the bush. Patches is digging a hole.

A screen door slams. Mrs. McCracken stands on her back porch, holding Dwight White. "Kids!" Mrs. McCracken calls. "Can you please tell Patches to stop that digging!"

"I'm sorry, Mrs. McCracken!" I call, 'cause Patches can't talk.

Just then Patches darts out, right into me. Oof!

"Oh, you bad dog!" Patches doesn't look sorry one bit.

Jack grabs hold of the leafy leash. "Got you!" Patches wags his tail like he just did something really good.

"Sorry, Mrs. McCracken. My sister let Patches get loose."

Mrs. McCracken gives Jack a sweet ol' smile. "Well, aren't you a wonderful big brother to help her?" She makes Dwight White give Jack a wave goodbye.

Fishsticks.

"And what happened to your hair?" Jack says as we walk home.

I pat my head. Hmm. Jack and I keep walking and then he says, "See what I mean, Lola? Trouble."

9. DINNER OF DOOM

"WANT TO PLAY BLANKET OF Doom?" I ask Jack.

"That's for little kids," Jack says. "Anyway, the guest bed is covered with Mom's stuff. And anyway, I have to go rake Mrs. Osborne's leaves."

"Can I at least help you? Please? Ohpleaseohpleaseohplease. I'll be grown up."

Jack thinks about it.

"Okay," he says.

Just then, who should come winging back into

the kitchen but Dad. Dear old Dad. And he's carrying *Building Codes Illustrated*, his most favorite book. He's got a big black ink mark on his face and a pile of tracing papers under his arm.

I head for the door. "Bye, Dad. I'm going to help Jack."

"Lola, come here right now," Dad says.

"But Dad . . . I want to help Jack."

"Gotta go!" Jack hollers and bounces out the door like a runaway basketball.

Fishsticks. It's a lot more fun being a grown-up–style kid than a regular one.

"Lola, did you tell Jessie Chavez that we would watch their dog during Thanksgiving break?"

I hang my head 'cause it weighs me down like a heavy pumpkin. "She asked me, and I wanted . . ."

Dad sighs. "Oh, Lola. We have so much going on at home. All the relatives coming. Mom's rush project. And I have a new job." He waves *Building Codes Illustrated* around.

"I promise I'll be a big kid and take care of Maizy and Barkley."

Dad's eyebrows fly up. And I notice one's got ink in it.

"Did you say Barkley, too? The Andersons' dog?"

My face gets hot as popcorn oil. "Well . . ."

Dad's face must be hot also. It turns red. Real red, like beets.

"Dad, I promise I will take care of those dogs and they won't get in your way ONE BIT. And guess what? It's only dogs, not cats."

"That is not an excuse, young lady. You should have asked."

Oh no. "I'm sorry, Dad." I feel some tears stinging away in my eyeballs. I stare at the floor. There goes an ant. Poor ol' ant. Maybe it ran away from home.

Dad sighs. "Okay, Lola. Let's take care of that knot. That's one problem you can solve right now."

BRRRING! That phone is sure loud.

"Stay right there," Dad says in a yellish voice to me. "Hello? . . . Oh, hi, Penny. Happy Thanksgiving to you, too. . . . Yes, yes, it's fine. . . . Yes, we'd be delighted to take care of Barkley. . . . No, no, it's not a problem. . . . All right, then. Bye, now."

Dad turns to me. "Well," is all he has to say. Except: "Upstairs!"

I march up the stairs with Dad right behind me like Weirdo Wolf who lived under Jack's bed only not really.

"All right, where's your hairbrush, Lola?"

"I lost it."

"Then we'll use Mom's."

Fishsticks. I drag my feet into their bathroom and open Mom's drawer. And there it is. Mom's mean ol', bright blue, turn-a-poodle-into-a-collie brush. I unloose my hair from the ponytail, take the brush, and glide it over my curls. The underneath part is still all tangled up. And the knot is hiding in there like an escaped criminal.

"Are you sure you're brushing it well?" Dad gives me a crooked eye.

I brush it more and more and more on the top. And guess what? My hair starts going wild! Even from my own eyeballs I can see it sticking up.

"Okay, okay, that's enough brushing," Dad says. He grabs the brush right out of my hand and that's bad manners. After he sticks it back in the drawer, he takes a look at my head. "Does Mom spray it or something?"

"Nope. Hairspray is for adults because Lord knows it stings when it gets in your face."

Dad's cell phone starts ringing. He answers.

"Hello? Oh, hi, honey. No, everything's fine here. Okay, three hundred and fifty degrees for an hour? All right. Love you, too."

"BYE, MOM!" I holler.

Dad rushes out of the bathroom.

"Lola, maybe you could get your head wet or something?"

"But Dad, I'll catch my death of a cold!"

"Then the baseball cap, Lola. Your mother will be home in an hour, and . . ." Dad gives me an Out of Gas look.

"Don't worry, Dad!" I say. I race past him down the hall and I find my baseball cap in my room. It's kind of tight on account of my pile of hair.

Downstairs, Dad is chopping vegetables at the counter. He looks at my head, but I think he sees carrots or cucumbers because he keeps chopping away.

"Want me to set the table?" I ask, helpful as I can be.

"That would be terrific, Lola," Dad says. And then he sings,

*"When I see you walking in the sunshine, my dear,
everything is absolutely, perfectly clear.
I love you. Yes, I love you."*

Ding dong. I run to the door to get it. It's Amanda, Jessie, and her Bammy, along with Maizy and Barkley, two bags of dog food, a stack of dog food cans, two bowls, two leashes, and a whole lot of barking. Oh, and a long list of dos and don'ts.

"Let's just bring them around to the backyard," I say, lickety-quick. "Patches is already back there."

"Are you sure they're ultra-safe?" Jessie asks.

"Sure, I'm sure."

After I say goodbye, I run back into the kitchen. Dad is still singing. He glances up and sees the dogs running around in the yard but he just keeps singing.

One whole hour later Mom comes bustling in with a bolt of fabric, and then Jack comes home, too. Mom has a piece of glittery thread hanging from her shoulder. Jack has leaves stuck in his hair. And they both look tired out like old bunnies. The dogs were asleep under the kitchen table. Now Patches thumps his tail, Maizy barks, and Barkley trots over to sniff Mom's hand.

Mom stares at them. "What?"

"I'm really sorry, Mom," I say. "I promised Amanda and Jessie that I would watch their dogs during Thanksgiving break."

Mom closes her eyes.

"Mom?"

She keeps her eyes shut.

"Honey?" Dad asks.

"I'm too tired and hungry to think," Mom says.

We sit down at the table that looks great. Because I made it all look nice. Even Amanda would just love it.

"Lola, please take off your hat at dinner," Mom says.

Fishsticks. I zloop it off. BOING.

"That's going to need a good brushing," Mom says. "Right after bath."

"Hmm," Dad says. "She did give it a good brushing. I watched her."

"That's my hair," Mom says. "There's a whole curly layer underneath. Tangles galore."

Dad serves us some steaming zucchini soufflé that is my favorite food in the whole world. We also have salad, and I like the tiny bits of carrots even though Mom doesn't cut them like that.

"Can I go first?" I ask. Every night we play a game. We go around the table and say two things about our day. Everyone else has to guess which one is true and which one is a ball-face lie. The winner gets to go next.

"I don't want to play," Jack says.

"What do you mean?" Mom and Dad say at the exact same time. We all stare at Jack like he's a big green bug that flew through the window.

"I'm a big kid. I have a job to help out the family. And big kids don't play games."

"Jack," Mom says. "That's very nice that you want to help our family. But why do you think you need to help out?"

"Because you and Dad work all the time to make ends meet," Jack says. "And Lola is always causing trouble. So that's why."

Mom's and Dad's mouths drop open, *plip, plop*.

"I am NOT just a little kid," I say. "And I'm NEVER going to like you EVER again, Jack Zuckerman. You are the WORST brother in the world."

"Lola, upstairs, now," Mom says. "And dessert is cancelled."

And that's how I went straight to a bath and no dessert.

I wash and condition my hair, and later I brush it with Mom staring her eyeballs right into my brain. Then she takes a turn with brushing but when she gets going good, I scream. Just a weensy ouchy-wa-wa scream.

"Lola Katherine Zuckerman," Mom says. And she

wags her finger at me. "Don't you understand? By ignoring a problem, you're not going to make it go away."

"But it hurts!" I bawl.

"Stop being a baby!" Jack yells outside the bathroom door.

"John Anthony Zuckerman!" Mom hollers back. "That is NOT helpful."

Mom turns to me. "Lola, I simply don't have time right now for this. I want you to take responsibility for your hair. If you can't, we're heading straight to the hair salon to get it cut short. AFTER I get this dress order finished."

"Okay," I say in an eensy-weensy voice.

And when it's time for bed, I think that I don't even like chocolate ice cream anyway. Maybe.

10. HALF DAY OF SCHOOL, FULL DAY OF TROUBLE

AS SOON AS I GET TO SCHOOL,
I take out my sloppy ol' braid that I gave myself
at the crack of dawn this morning. BOING. My hair
dances on my head on account of getting free. The
morning bell rings.

"Gobble, gobble!" Harvey Baxter yells. "Look at
me! I'm a turkey!" Gwendolyn Swanson-Carmichael
yells at him to stop. I wonder if I'm going to get a
haircut like Harvey Baxter.

"Harvey, Gwendolyn," Mrs. D. says. Then she

takes a swig from her travel coffee mug.

BUZZ.

CRACKLE.

"Good morning, boys and girls," Principal McCoy says. "Please remember that school will be dismissed at noon today. All after-school activities are cancelled. I want to wish you all a happy and healthy Thanksgiving!"

I'm lined up, waiting to sharpen my pencils. I love a sharp pencil, even on a half day. Amanda and Savannah come rushing up.

"Was your mom happy to see Barkley? What did

your mom say about that?" Amanda chews on her lip.

I cross my fingers behind my back. "She was one hundred percent happy to see Barkley. And Maizy."

"Whew! I thought she would say no more dogs!" Amanda grins.

"My mom LUH-HUVS dogs," I say. "And even if she doesn't have time to come to our class party, that's because she has eight and a half more dresses to sew." And my whole face itches. 'Cause I'm a big ol' liar and I'm probably going to get killed by Mom if she has time to kill me if she takes a sewing break. Maizy and Barkley barked all night long, and Patches howled back. It was kind of like a dog concert.

Once everyone gets here, Mrs. D. says, "Good morning, Tootsie Pops!" She does the roll call and then she announces, "Morning meeting!"

We run to the carpet because we want to sit next to Mrs. D.

"Today we're going to make Thanksgiving Day cards for our relatives and friends."

Sam's hand shoots up. "When are we having our party?"

"After recess," Mrs. D. says.

At recess, I line up for the swings with Savannah.

Harvey Baxter points at my head. "You look like an alien!"

I pat my hair knot and stick out my tongue. "So! I'll zap you with my alien laser." It's handy having an

older brother. I know just what to say.

But my face feels droopy. Savannah puts her arm around me. "I like your hair style," Savannah says.

"It's not really a style," I say. It's no fun having a hair knot. And getting all my hair chopped off is going to be no fun, too.

"Well, I think you're lucky to have curly hair," Savannah says. "My mom curls my hair and mousses it up and sprays it on picture day. That's N-O fun."

I pat my curly ol' head. And I give Savannah a hug.

When it's our turn for the swings, me and Savannah have a contest to see who can go the highest. I don't have to keep slowing down and pushing up my glasses like Savannah does. I slow myself down and let Savannah win. It gives me a good feeling inside. I bow to the cheering crowds and get a gold ribbon for goodness. After recess, we kids go pouring into the classroom.

Ari's dad is there. He gives Ari a high five.

Fishsticks. My dad doesn't have time for anything fun. He's making lots of stuff ahead of time today, like cheese sauce and brine. I never ate brine before. I hope. He also forgot to wash the cloth napkins and Mom said no to paper towels.

"Mommy!" Amanda yells.

"Hello, sweets," Amanda's mom says. My tummy feels slimy like leftover salad. And my heart feels flat as a burnt pancake.

"Did you bring the pumpkin muffins?" Amanda asks.

I eavesdrop in case she forgot, and Amanda wings out of the room, bawling like a little tiny baby that I have to burp.

"Of course I did," Mrs. Anderson says.

"All right, Jellybeans," Mrs. D. says. "Take a seat. We're going to make Thanksgiving Day cards."

"You're trying to get us under control." Harvey Baxter pogos over to his desk.

"Yes, I am." Mrs. D. hands out brown and orange paper.

"When everyone is finished with your Thanksgiving Day cards, it will be time to enjoy the nice feast prepared by Mrs. Anderson and Mr. Shapiro."

Sam is the first one to finish his card. He wears his paper plate as a hat. Everyone lines up at the Thanksgiving buffet. Mrs. Anderson and Mr. Shapiro help the kids to not slop the cranberry sauce everywhere and only take one turkey-shaped sugar cookie.

"What key won't open any door?" Mr. Shapiro asks. "A turkey!" He's got lots of funny jokes like that.

"Lola," Mrs. Anderson says when I get up close. "Your mom told me that Barkley was a surprise. I know you meant well, sweetie. But next time you really need to let the moms and dads in on the action. Okay?"

I nod. One time Patches ate a whole bowl of brussels sprouts right off the table. Now I know how he felt. No matter how hard I try to be a grown-up kid, I just keep on being a smelly rat baby.

Mrs. Anderson leans forward and whispers, "Now, don't be sad, Lola. You're such a good friend. It's much nicer knowing our pets will be taken care of by friends."

Next, I sit on the carpet next to Amanda and Savannah. "Barkley likes to be petted, but not when he's eating," Amanda says. "And he likes wet food mixed in with his dry."

"Fishsticks," I say. "Anything else?"

"Barkley will eat food off the counter if you don't watch him, and if he does, he'll be a real stinker."

"A toot stinker?"

"Yes."

"I'd better make a list," I say. I shove the rest of my turkey sugar cookie in my mouth and run to my desk.

I grab a piece of paper and my watermelon-smelling pencil. I write

- Pet Barkley
- But not when he's eating
- Mix wet dog food and dry food for Barkley
- Don't let him eat off the counter

"Is that it?"

Mrs. Anderson comes over and looks at the list. "Excellent," she says. "Amanda, it's time to say goodbye. We have to catch our flight."

"Gumdrops, let's wish Amanda a wonderful Thanksgiving in Cancún!" Mrs. D. says. She lifts her travel mug.

"Bye, Amanda!" all the kids say.

I hug Amanda goodbye. I whisper, "Don't worry about Barkley. I'll take good care of him."

After our party, we have Independent Reading. But I keep reading the same line over and over.

And instead of it saying *Margaret walked down the country lane*, it says *Bald Lola got put in jail by her parents for ruining Thanksgiving*.

Pretty soon it's time for all the kids to pack up and go. Mrs. D. dismisses everyone from the classroom alphabetically. "Last but not least, Lola," Mrs. D. says with a friendly smile. "It was very sweet of you to take care of Amanda's dog. It's a lot of work. You probably made Amanda feel very happy about her trip."

I don't feel sweet. I feel sour as a pickle. Sour as a rhubarb. Sour as a rhubarb and pickle sandwich.

11. TAM-O' UH-OH

DAD HAS A SOY SAUCE LOOK ON his face at the bus stop.

"Hi, Dad!"

"Lola Katherine Zuckerman," he says. Uh-oh. All three names again.

"We have some big holes in the backyard."

I hang my snarled-up head. "Sorry, Dad. I thought it would be okay since you and Mom love animals."

"Oh, Lola, we do love animals. And I know you

did this out of the kindness of your heart. But Lola, Mom and I told you that we have a lot of extra work right now. My company has been really generous about letting me work from home this week. And we're hosting Thanksgiving."

Dad and I walk up the road. In the kitchen, Patches, Maizy, and Barkley are playing tug of war with one of Jack's gigantic smelly socks.

"What's your plan, Lola?"

"I'll give them plenty of exercise before the relatives arrive. And I'll set up a Pet Palace in the basement so they'll be as happy as can be."

The Soy Sauce look leaves Dad's face, a little at least.

"That might work," Dad says. "What we don't want to do is create more work for Mom. Not when she's in the middle of her big project. Right?"

"Right," I say.

"Why don't you start by tidying up your hair? It looks like it got a little messy at school," Dad says.

I zip upstairs and brush my hair. Sort of. Then I do the hokey pokey, and wish I was in Cancún with Amanda. I spy with my big ol' eye a beret that Grandma got for me. I stick that beret right on top of my head and squish all my snarls inside and *bam, bam, bam* back downstairs.

I grab Barkley by the collar. "I think I'll take them for a walk."

"I don't think you can take all of them at once," Dad says. "Why don't you take Maizy and Barkley?"

"But . . ." And then I shut my "but" up.

I follow Dad to the kitchen and get Maizy's and Barkley's leashes. I can hear Mom's sewing machine *rrr*ing away in the guest room. I fasten their leashes to their collars, and Barkley snatches that beret right off my head. I go back out the door just as Jack is getting home on account of his half day being bigger than mine.

"Hey, Barkster," Jack gives Barkley a friendly scratch. "Why does he have a hat in his mouth?"

I sigh loud so he knows I had a hard day. "It's a long story."

Barkley is excited to be back in his old neighborhood. It's very hard holding on to the leash. Maizy is scared to be here. She thinks every blowing leaf is a mini-monster out to get her. It takes me four hundred hours to take four steps. Too bad Patches isn't here to make her feel better.

Mrs. McCracken is sitting on her front porch cuddling with Dwight White.

"More dogs?" she calls out.

"Yep! I'm watching them for my friends. It's Maizy. And Barkley. Remember him?"

"How could I forget?" Mrs. McCracken says in a Dry Pancake voice. "What's he got in his mouth?"

"My beret that my grandma gave me."

For some reason my voice gets all wobbly.

Mrs. McCracken looks at me for a minute. Mrs. McCracken has a Maybe-Style smile on her face. "Dogs really like hats."

"Yes. I told my friends I would watch their dogs while they go on deluxe vacations and I stay home, but they keep causing trouble. Not my friends. The dogs. And my mom and my dad are both really busy. My mom isn't making her broccoli with a cheese sauce and so my dad has to make all of the extra stuff and the turkey and . . . Hey, Mrs. McCracken, are you cooking a turkey?"

"No, not this year," Mrs. McCracken says. She looks kind of sad. I try to think of something to say.

I feel the back of my head. The knot is now about the size of Rhode Island.

"Hold on there." Mrs. McCracken rushes off, old-people style, and then she comes out with a hat shaped like a big circle with a pom-pom on top.

"It's called a tam-o'-shanter or a tam hat."

I put it on my head. "It looks darling!" Mrs. McCracken says. She smiles a regular-sized smile. I smile at Mrs. McCracken. And Barkley wags his tail.

"That's his way of saying sorry," I explain. "Do you forgive him?"

"I guess I do."

"And Patches too?"

"Patches too." This time Mrs. McCracken's smile is as sweet as pie. Not lemon pie. Coconut cream pie.

Then I start to wonder. What is Dwight White going to do all by his lonesome at Thanksgiving? And Mrs. McCracken, too.

12. READY, SET, COOK!

DAD SAYS IT'S A DOWN-TO-THE-
Wire afternoon. That means me and Jack have to be
on our best behavior while Dad runs around and
around the kitchen. Timers are going off and things
are bubbling on the stove. It smells like butter and
cinnamon and sugar and warm bread. I run upstairs
to wash my hands, take off Mrs. McCracken's tam-
o'-shanter, and wet down the puffed-up part of my
hair.

Mom comes out one time and says one helpful

hint about how Dad doesn't have to hand chop all the celery and onion for the stuffing. Then Dad says if she wants to do it, she's more than welcome to. And guess what? He doesn't yell it but I hear a yell stuck in his throat. Mom says he's doing a fine job. She gives him a kiss and me a kiss and Jack a kiss, and she heads on back to her *rrrrr-rrrrr*-sewing.

Chop-chop-choppety-chop.

Jack's job is to mash the potatoes. Tomorrow we'll heat them up. He pounds away at them. "Take that!" he yells.

It's my job to set the big dining room table. I do it as fast as I can because I can't take my eye off Patches, Maizy, and Barkley. I've thrown the ball to them so many times my arm feels like it's loose in the socket.

At dinnertime, we have pizza in the kitchen, and Dad nods off at the table. Me and Jack bring the pizza box to the recycling bin in the garage. Then we wipe all the crumbs off the table.

I bring the dogs down to the basement and tell them a good-night story.

"'Twas the night before Thanksgiving, and all through the house, not a creature was stirring, not even you three dogs. You kind of missed your own mom and dad, but you were mostly fine and a little bit glad. You had each other, three best friends, what more could be better? And that is the end."

Barkley whined when I finished my story. "I know, Barkley. I miss Amanda, too."

Then Maizy howled. "Jessie, too. And Savannah. But we'll get to see them soon. Now I want the three of you to snuggle in tight and be good dogs."

I leave the dogs to cuddle together, and I head upstairs. Mom sews buttons on a bright green Lola dress while I take my bath. Then I brush my teeth, and kind of, sort of brush my hair. And Mom doesn't say a word. Because we both know: If I don't get this knot out, it's Lola Chopperman for me.

I climb into bed and wait for Dad to come in and tell me a Chuncle story.

But he doesn't. And he still doesn't after I count to ninety-six.

Jack comes in. "Do you know what monsters put on their Thanksgiving table? Knives, forks, and goons."

"That scares me." I pull the covers to my chin.

"Hmm. Why did the turkey cross the road?"

I pull the covers up higher. "A monster was chasing him?"

"No, it was the chicken's day off!"

I laugh, and Jack laughs, too.

13. PILING ON THE PIES

THE NEXT MORNING I WAKE UP
to the smell of YUM. I hurry downstairs to let the
dogs out in the backyard to do their business and
have a dog playdate. While I'm out there, I find my
beret where Barkley must have dropped it. After
I pull it on my head, I use a shovel to fill in some
dog holes, and I pick up some dog doo with special
plastic bags. PEE-YOO. I bring it to the special can
in the garage and put away the shovel.

That's when I hear somebody yelling. I run back
inside.

"Where's my grandkids? Where'd you hide my grandbabies?"

Grampy and Granny Coogan come through the door hooting and hollering. They wear matching white cowboy hats and matching sweatshirts that say "Texas A & M."

Granny Coogan takes off her hat. She has red hair just like Mom, only with lots of silvery parts. She's plump—that's when you're pretty and lumpy. Grampy Coogan has big ears and likes to whittle.

"Holy Guacamole! My little Lola grew up!" Granny Coogan says. She gives me a kiss on my head and a hug. "How's my peanut?"

"I grew a whole inch since summer, Granny Coogan," I say.

"That's wunnerful," Granny Coogan says. "And guess what I brought you, Lola dear? A pumpkin pie! Because who makes the best pumpkin pie in the whole country?"

"You do, Granny Coogan," I say.

"You got that right," Grampy Coogan says.

"Brought two pies, frozen solid, but they're starting to thaw out. I wouldn't want to let my Lola down. Now, where is that brother of yours?" Granny Coogan asks.

"Here I am." Jack barges in. He has been helping Dad bring in the extra chairs from the garage.

"Who's that big fellow?" Grampy Coogan says.

"It's Jack," I tell him.

"He's gone and grown as big as an oak tree!"

Jack stands up very straight.

"Bye," Dad calls. "I'll be back soon with Grandma from the train station."

"Got any coffee, dear?" Grampy Coogan asks Mom.

"Sure, Dad." Mom is grinning so big. She pours him a cup. Grampy Coogan drinks coffee all day. It doesn't make him hyper.

Grampy looks out the window into the backyard. "You got yourself a few more hound dogs?" he asks. The dogs are running around and around and barking.

"It's a long story," Mom says. "But Lola, you know what to do."

"Sugar, why are you wearing that beret? Can't we get a look at that bee-yoo-ti-ful hair of yours?" Granny Coogan asks. "It's the exact same color mine was at your age. I just love it."

Mom gives me The Look.

Uh-oh. I think fast. I say quickly, "I'll be right back, Granny."

The dogs sure don't want to come inside. But they follow me because I have three pieces of deli ham that I'm holding way up high. I bring the dogs down to the basement and give each one of them a slice. Even though Barkley tries to take them all. That stinker.

"I expect you all to be on your best behavior. We have company."

Patches scratches behind his ears. Barkley slumps onto the floor. Maizy barks.

At the top of the stairs, I say, "I think I've made myself clear."

Dad is just pulling into the driveway with Grandma. I run outside. "Grandma!" I yell. Grandma steps out of the car in her high-heeled shoes. She wears all black because that's what people from Brooklyn do.

"Oh, Lola," Grandma says. "You're wearing your beret that I brought you from Paris. How wonderful!"

"Yep," I say and give my beret a pat. It's a little wettish.

Grandma hands me a package. I hope there's fudge inside but it's a ribbon. A red velvet one that Amanda Anderson would love.

"That will look just splendid in your hair, Lola dear," she says.

"Thank you, Grandma," I say.

Grandma has a box in her hand.

"My darling girl, guess what I have in this box?" Grandma says.

"Chocolate cake?" I ask with wishful thinking. Wishful thinking is when you tell a whopper but just to yourself.

"No, pumpkin pie! Who makes the best pumpkin pie in the whole world?"

"You do, Grandma," I say.

"Lola, my darling girl," Grandma says. "I can't

wait to serve you a slice of my delicious pumpkin pie!"

"I can't wait, too," I say-lie.

Poor, poor Grandma. She doesn't realize that her own granddaughter is a fibber. I hate ribbons. And HER pumpkin pie is the one that tastes just like licking a candle.

Lying is bad. So is getting caught. And I'm about to get caught. Because only one pumpkin pie can be the best.

14. ME TO THE RESCUE

I TAKE OFF THE BERET UPSTAIRS
and tie up my hair in my new big fat red ribbon. Jack
says I look like a Christmas present, and that isn't
nice.

For about a hundred years, the adults sit around
talking. We eat hors d'oeuvres. Those are fancy
snacks pronounced ORR DURVS. Grandma taught
me. Not horse doovers like Grampy Coogan says.

Me and Jack sit near the black olives. Jack wears
a red tie that matches Dad's red tie. And Grandma's
eyes get all wet and she takes a picture of them.

Dad gives her a hug because sometimes your mom gets sad and the only thing that makes her feel better is a hug.

Grampy and Granny Coogan and Grandma are all around the same amount of oldness. They have lots of catching up to do since they never celebrate Thanksgiving together.

I wait and wait and wait for a moment to bust in and tell them my grown-up–kid idea. But they never take a breath. So I just barge in and tell them my idea.

"Lola, that's a wonderful suggestion," Mom and Dad say. Dad grabs his jacket and heads out the door. "Be right back!"

While Dad is gone, we head into the kitchen and start bringing bowls and plates to the table. The food smells buttery and spicy and yummy. Last but not least, I carry in Mom's basket of rolls.

The table is loaded down with food. I take a seat between my two grandmas, Zuckerman and Coogan.

Just then, Dad comes in with Mrs. McCracken. She's carrying a pie plate. Mrs. McCracken's eyes are smiling and so are her lips.

"Thank you for inviting me," Mrs. McCracken says. She holds out her pie plate.

"Oh, Mrs. McCracken, you didn't have to bring anything!" Mom says.

"I was already baking," Mrs. McCracken says. "Pumpkin pie."

Jack and I look at each other. Pumpkin pie again!

"How lovely!" Mom says.

Mrs. McCracken comes in and joins the old people at the Thanksgiving table. They chat about the good old days. Dad helps Mom, Jack, and me carry the rest of the stuff to the table.

Finally, it's time for all of us to sit down.

I send Jack a message. I am SO a grown-up kid. Even if I have a secret hair knot. And a pile of dogs to watch.

Everyone eats turkey, and stuffing, and mashed potatoes, and salad and broccoli with a cheese sauce. Everyone eats cranberry sauce that is shaped just like a can. I made it myself. Finally it's time for dessert.

Pumpkin Pie.

Pumpkin Pie.

Pumpkin Pie!

The pies are on the counter. Everyone lines up, and everyone takes three slices of pie. Everyone goes back to the table. Everyone doesn't look at anyone.

First I take a bite of Granny Coogan's pumpkin pie. Mmmm, it's good.

"Well, Lola," Granny Coogan says. "How is it?"

"It's yummy!" I say.

Next, I take a bite of Grandma's pumpkin pie. Eww. It tastes just like I remember. Like licking a bad ol' candle. And I should know cause I did that once.

"Lola, darling?" Grandma asks. "How was mine?"

"Delicious," I lie.

"And whose is the best?" Both grandmothers ask me that at the exact same time.

Ooh, my tummy hurts. So does my head. Lying

is bad. So is getting caught. And boy, oh, boy, I am caught.

My mouth opens just like the salmon on ice at Fred's Fresh Fish Market. I have to tell the truth.

"Hold on there!" Mrs. McCracken says. "You have to try mine, too!"

I take a bite out of Mrs. McCracken's pumpkin pie. It is the fluffiest, most delicious pumpkin pie. My eyes open wide 'cause I never knew pumpkin pie could taste so good. I say, "Mmm, mmm, that's good pie!"

"Yeah," Jack grunts. Grunting is saying yum with a growl.

"Mrs. McCracken," I say in my Announcement voice. "Your pumpkin pie is the best. The best pumpkin pie contest is over!"

"Yahoo!" Jack yells.

Granny Coogan and Grandma get all pink in the face. They look at each other and burst out laughing.

Granny Coogan takes a bite of Mrs. McCracken's pie. Her eyes get very wide. "Y'all know what? This pumpkin pie beats mine to Kalamazoo and back!"

Grandma takes a bite. She closes her eyes. "Heavenly," she says. Mrs. McCracken grins really big.

"Maybe you should try chocolate mousse

pie next year," Dad suggests to Grandma. "They probably sell that at Kling's Bakery."

Jack and I look at each other. Grandma doesn't bake her own pies. She buys them! No wonder they taste like licking a candle.

"And y'all have never tried my world-famous blueberry pie! It'll knock your socks off!" Granny Coogan says.

Jack and I smile at each other. It's going to be great to have a dessert that isn't pumpkin pie!

Aaarrrrrr-OOOOOO!

Aaarrrrrr-OOOOOO!

I drop my fork. "Barkley!"

I run to the stairs. "You be quiet down there!" I yell. "Do you hear me?"

Aaarrrrrr-OOOOOO!

Aaarrrrrr-OOOOOO!

"They didn't hear you!" Jack says.

I open the door a smidge.

"Lola, be—" Mom says.

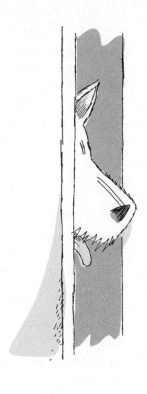

"I said be quiet!" I say through the smidge. A wet snout pops through the opening. "Go back in there!"

But Maizy pushes that door right open! She darts out, followed by Barkley, followed by Patches!

15. NOT EXACTLY MY PLAN

"PATCHES!" I YELL. I CHASE
after Patches! Patches chases Barkley and Barkley
chases Maizy. Maizy is like a white streak of melting
vanilla ice cream going around and around the
Thanksgiving table.

Jack jumps up. "Patches!" he yells.

"Well, snap my stays and call me granny!"
Granny Coogan exclaims. "You've got a circus in
here!"

"Lola, grab him!" Dad shouts.

"I'm trying!" I yell. I jump for Patches and I get his tail but it slides out of my fingers. Around and around the table he goes, chasing the other dogs. "It's a good thing Dwight White didn't come over!" I call to Mrs. McCracken.

Barkley barks. *RUFF! RUFF! RUFF!* He knocks against the table and Mom's piece of pumpkin pie slides off and right into her lap.

Finally I get those dogs corralled and back in the basement. Mom heads upstairs to change her pants.

I clear the table along with Jack and he just shakes his head at me. "Trouble, trouble, and more trouble," is what he says.

Afterward, we go back into the living room to drink tea and coffee, except me and Jack just lie on the floor like stuffed pillows.

"I plumb forgot!" Granny Coogan reaches into a shopping bag. "I brought you each a Texas A & M baseball hat."

"Thank you, Granny Coogan," Jack and I say. Jack slaps his right on his head.

"Lola, why don't you take off the ribbon and try it on?" Dad asks.

"You don't have to," Granny Coogan says in a rush.

"Oh, do go ahead," Grandma says.

Slowly I untie the ribbon. Easy, easy. BOING! My curly whirly hair springs out like a wild animal.

"Lola's got a hair knot the size of New York City," Grandma says.

"That's a hair knot the size of Texas, I reckon," Granny Coogan says.

BOING!

16. LOTS OF KNOTS

MOM PILES A BUNCH OF
Thanksgiving food into a genuine recyclable
container for Mrs. McCracken. We get her all hugged
up and then Dad walks her home.

Even though I tell Grandma and Granny that I'm
just going to get my hair chopped off into a crew cut
like Grampy's, they say I should give it another try.

They must mean another cry.

Because it's going to hurt.

Grandma and Granny Coogan and me climb the

stairs. In the bathroom, I run myself a bath. I add some of my favorite bath bubbles.

I wash my hair with Go Bananas Shampoo. I condition it with Berry Glad To Meet You conditioner.

"I suggest you separate it into sections and brush it," Grandma says. "That's how I did it when I was a girl."

"Oh, I wouldn't do that, Zelda!" Granny says. "She has my hair. Best way is to just run that brush right through."

"Well!" Grandma says. "I think her hair is a lot like mine!"

Uh-oh. My knot is causing all kinds of problems.

"I think my hair is half and half," I tell them. "It's half Granny and half Grandma!"

The three of us look at each other. I give them both a smile. "May I have the brush, please?" I ask.

Grandma hands me the bright blue brush. Granny Coogan smiles at me and nods.

I part my hair down the middle, 'cause that's two sections at least. Then I suck in a bunch of air. I scrunch up my face. The first bunch of air goes right out of me so I have to suck in some more air.

And I start brushing my hair. First, I brush not

too hard. I sort of brush the air. But then my brush touches my hair. Just a little at first. Then a little harder. I start brushing at that big ol' hair knot. Grrr!

"Take that," I tell it.

I brush and brush and brush. And I brush so much, my arm gets worn out. But I make it keep brushing and brushing.

I brush and brush until my hair flattens like spaghetti almost. I know the hair knot is still hiding there. So I take a deep breath. OW! That brush snags through my hair knot. Some of my hair comes right out! I put that hair on the side of the tub.

Granny whistles. "Would you look at that?"

"Oh my," Grandma says.

The next time I give that knot a brush, it's gone! I did it!

I'm never going to skip over the knots EVER again. Maybe.

17. BEDTIME BUGABOO

WHEN IT'S TIME FOR BED, I GET a big worry in my head. I know that Granny Coogan makes better pumpkin pie than Grandma. Granny also likes to grow up vegetables, and she lets me stir her chocolate pudding and doesn't yell when it splatters her new pink blouse.

But Grandma tells me stories about Brooklyn and Zelda the Zebra. She shows me how outfits go together. She takes me and Jack to Broadway shows and at intermission we overdo it at the snack bar.

All I do is cause trouble, trouble, trouble for

Dad and Mom. Maybe if I moved away, they wouldn't have to work so hard. Maybe I should just move in with Granny and Grampy. Or Grandma.

One of my grandmas is plump and cuddly and makes yummy food. One of them wears leopard dresses and sings show tunes.

But even though Jack's getting old and doesn't want to play Blanket of Doom with me, I'd be really, really sad if I only saw him at Thanksgiving.

I feel a tickle in the back of my throat.

Then it's a stingaling tickle. I start crying and carrying on.

Mom comes rushing in. "Lola, what's the matter, honey?"

"I can't decide!" I cry.

Jack comes barreling in. "You can't decide what?"

"Which grandma I should live with. Granny or Grandma."

Mom sits down on the side of my bed.

"Lola, what makes you think you

need to live with either one?"

There's a little knock at my door, and then Grandma comes in, and so does Dad and Grampy Coogan and Granny Coogan. My whole room is stuffed full of people.

"We heard that caterwaulin'," Grampy says. "What's up, Peaches?"

I look at my two grannies and hope that nobody gets fired up. "I don't know who to go live with. Jack told me that all I do is cause trouble, and I know he's right but I just can't help it."

"Who did you pick?" both my grannies ask at the exact same time.

"I can't decide. I love you both," I say.

"Lola," Mom says. She nestles in close. She smells like pumpkin pie and bath salts. "Do you remember the time I only wanted to eat strawberries?"

I nod.

Grampy laughs. "Oh, boy! I sure do."

"Well, it probably wasn't fun for Granny and Grampy to just feed me strawberries."

"And remember when I told you about Chuncle getting stuck in the heating vent?" Dad says.

"I think it was you," Grandma says.

"You see, no matter how much trouble we might have caused our parents, they still loved us. Just like Dad and I will always love you. We would never want you to be anywhere but exactly where you are. At home with us."

"Even though you're kind of busy," I say.

"That won't be forever, you know."

"I knew that," Jack says. "'Cause you reminded me already."

Mom gives me a big hug. And pretty soon everybody is hugging everybody else.

"Lola," Granny says. "I'm real sorry I asked you who you would pick."

"Me, too," Grandma says. "I think you have enough love in your heart for all of us."

I grin at my two grandmas and my Grampy Coogan. "I do," I say.

"Me, too," Jack says. "Even though I'm old."

18. FRIENDSHIP CIRCLE

MRS. D. WELCOMES US BACK.

Savannah has a bunch of new freckles, Jessie has her hair all braided up, and Sam has a real wishbone. Amanda has a sombrero.

"Lollipops," Mrs. D. says, "take out your journals. We're going to finish what we started in Writers' Workshop. Please write about what you were thankful for at Thanksgiving."

We kids go back to our desks and I take out my watermelon-smelling pencil. My page is still blank from before, but this time, I don't have to think for a minute. I know what to write.

This Thanksgiving I was thankful that Mom was able to get the pumpkin pie stains out of her brand new cream-colored trousers that originally cost $40 and that she got on sale for only $14 at Kale's Department Store because Lord knows it's hard to find a well-fitting pair of trousers these days. And at a reasonable price.

I was also thankful that Mrs. McCracken made the best pumpkin pie ever. Now the pie contest is over!

I'm also thankful that I was at home for Thanksgiving with my whole entire family.

I'm really, really thankful that I got the hair knot the size of Texas out of my hair.

Love,

Lola

All the kids turn in their journals. We run out for recess. Jessie tells us about getting her hair braided and getting an upset tummy. Savannah tells us about playing Mother May I with all her cousins. I swing on the swings, and Amanda tells me all about the big waves in Cancún.

Then we four sit in a friendship circle because it's sunny and golden like toast. I made that friendship circle up. In case you want to try it, you can. You just need friends and stuff to talk about.

"Maizy slept for a whole day after we picked her up," Jessie tells me.

I am peppery about that. "Well, she got lots of exercise."

"Barkley loved it on Cherry Tree Lane," Amanda says.

"He can come back for a visit anytime," I say. "As long as I ask Mom and Dad first."

The bell rings. Savannah and Jessie run away to line up. But Amanda Anderson and I say, "Ooga booga! Ooga! Booga!" And we give our secret Peanut Butter and Jelly handshake.

Don't Miss Lola's Other Adventures!

LAST-BUT-NOT-LEAST LOLA GOING GREEN

Meet Lola Zuckerman, whose name is a big problem, because she's always Z-for-Zuckerman last. Lola needs to win her class's Going Green contest to prove to her ex-best friend, Amanda Anderson, who goes first every single time, that while she may be last, she is certainly not least.

LAST-BUT-NOT-LEAST LOLA and the WILD CHICKEN

Lola wants to play with her best friend, Amanda, all by herself. But Amanda's neighbor, Jessie, and now the new girl, Savannah, want to be friends with Amanda, too. Will a class trip to Kookamut Farm and an encounter with a wild chicken help the four girls solve their problems? Maybe . . .

LAST-BUT-NOT-LEAST LOLA and the CUPCAKE QUEENS

Lola's problems are piling up like leaves. The lie she told is spiraling out of control, there aren't enough Cupcake Queens Halloween costumes for her and her three friends, and she's terrified that she'll forget her lines for the class play. What Lola needs is bravery, but can she find it when she's quivering like a leaf in the wind?